For Denise, for making things happen — TF

For Alma. With special thanks to Allan for increasing the pressure — IC

Based on an idea by Noa Karavan-Cohen

First published 2005 by Walker Books Ltd, 87 Vauxhall Walk, London SE11 5HJ   This edition published 2006   10 9 8 7 6 5 4 3 2 1
Text © 2005 Toby Forward   Illustrations © 2005 Izhar Cohen   The right of Toby Forward and Izhar Cohen to be identified as author and illustrator
respectively of this work has been asserted by them in accordance with the Copyright, Designs and Patents Act 1988   This book has been typset in Gararond
British Library Cataloguing in Publication Data: a catalogue record for this book is available from the British Library
ISBN-13: 978-1-4063-0162-5   ISBN-10: 1-4063-0162-0   www.walkerbooks.co.uk

WALKER BOOKS
AND SUBSIDIARIES
LONDON · BOSTON · SYDNEY · AUCKLAND

WHAT REALLY HAPPENED TO LITTLE RED RIDING HOOD

The Wolf's Story

Toby Forward   Izhar Cohen

NO, PLEASE. Look at me.
Would I LIE to you?
It was the old woman who started it.
I did *nothing* wrong. Would I?
We hit it off from the beginning.
    Not everyone likes a wolf, do they?
    Look at *you*.
    You're not certain.

Would you like to come and sit a bit
closer while I tell you about the kid?
I don't bite.
        No? Sure? Okay.
        Up to you.

Anyway, I did odd jobs for the old
woman.
Called her *Grandma.* We were close.
I put up shelves,
did the shopping,
tidied the garden.
I *even* altered her clothes –
sewed on buttons,
that sort of
thing.

I'm **versatile!**

Sort of a new wolf. Vegetarian cuisine a speciality. If I eat any more lettuce I'll turn green. But that's too much information.

Are you *sure* you wouldn't like to sit just a little closer?

EVERY WEEK the kid called, with a basket of toffee. I tell you, that toffee was so bad it made Grandma's teeth stick together. And you don't want toffee messing up your false teeth.

But Grandma looked forward to seeing the kid. She even made her a red cape, so she could see her coming.

Did **anyone** ever make me a cape?

Me, I didn't like the kid being there. She *never* spoke to me. She seemed nervous. Can you believe that? When Little Red was there I felt left out.

I tried to join in. I even offered to eat the toffee, and that stuff could ruin a wolf's good teeth! So you can see how I tried.

But they just ignored me.

THE DAY it happened was like this — I saw the kid coming with her big basket of toffee.
I was out looking for fresh herbs in the forest, and I *tried* to pass the time of day with her.

But she pretended not to know me and hurried on.
That's the sort of kid she is.

Like I'm frightening? Eh?

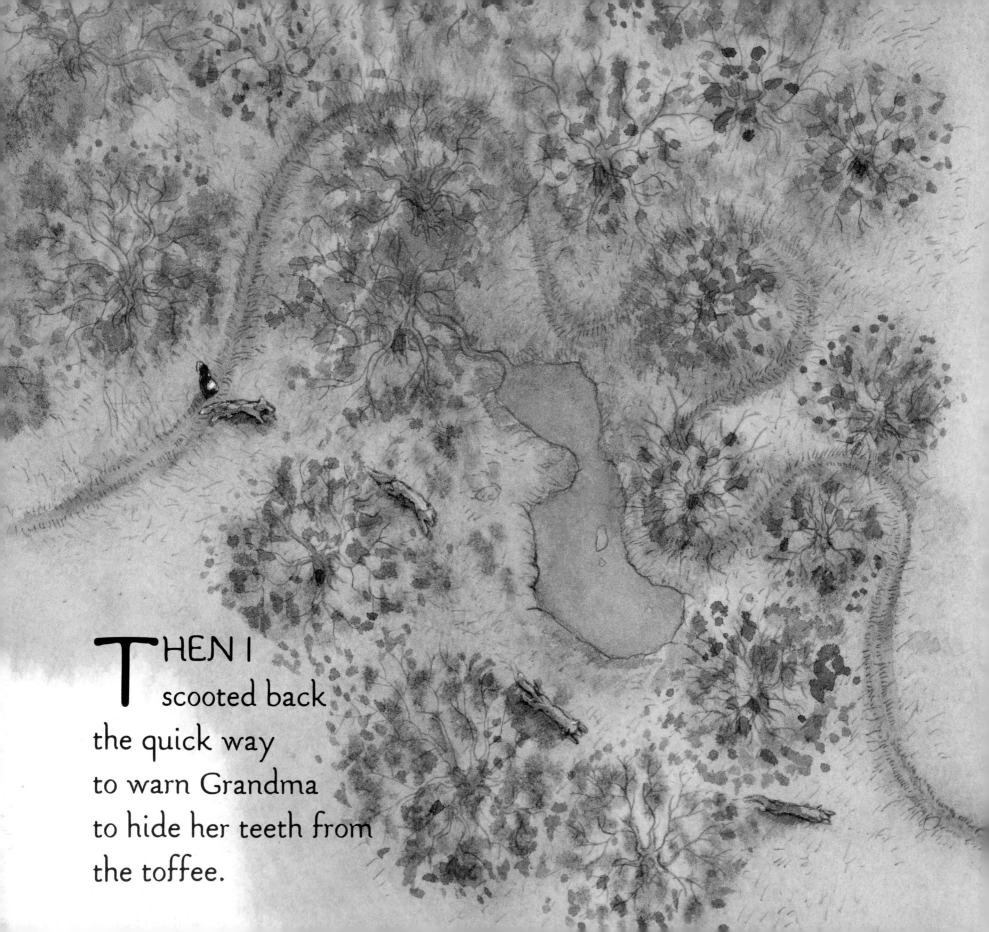

THEN I
scooted back
the quick way
to warn Grandma
to hide her teeth from
the toffee.

The kid always took a long time to get there. You know how *slow* kids are. When I got back, Grandma was reaching for her best dress in the wardrobe and couldn't reach the hook.

And this is the part where it all went wrong.

I TRIED to help her get it, but she fell over, right into the wardrobe. And, you know how it is – Grandma got a teeny tiny bump on the head that knocked her cold. And the kid was banging on the door.

All right. I panicked. It looked bad.

Not everyone trusts a wolf. I thought they might say I'd done something bad to Grandma.

ME?

Anyway, I shut the wardrobe, put the dress on – sort of thought I could cover it up, act like Grandma till she was better.

I have to admit, I don't have the best legs for a frock. So I jumped into the bed. Anyone would have thought I was Grandma.

THEN the kid came in and started acting strange. She was pretending to be scared again, and she wouldn't come close. *"Oh, Grandma,"* she said. *"What BIG eyes you have."*

"Got rid of my glasses," I told her. "I've got these new contacts. Really sore when you first put them in. Make *anyone's* eyes look big."

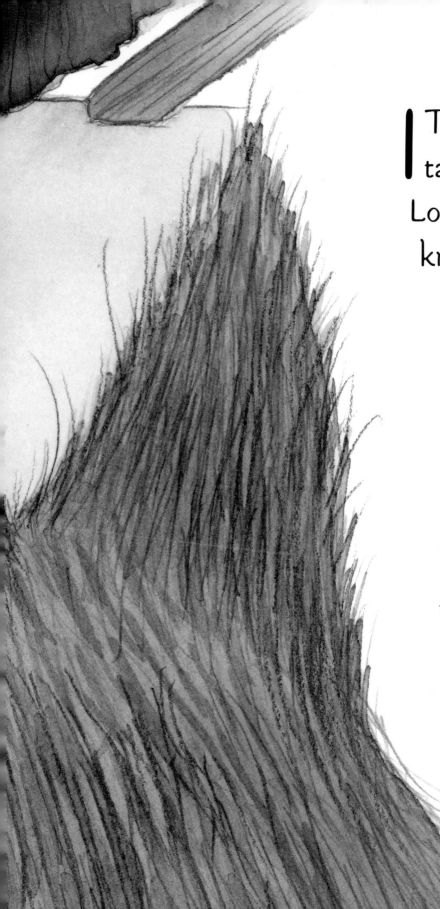

IT WAS the first time we'd had a talk, and she wasn't that bad, really. Looked good enough to eat, if you know what I mean.

"Oh, Grandma," she said.
"What **BIG** *ears you have."*

Now, these are good ears.
But I have to admit, they aren't a lot like Grandma's, and, of course, they're pretty furry as well.

"Oh, these old things," I said and changed the subject.

"Oh, Grandma," she said.
"What *BIG* teeth you have."

And this was what made it *worse...*

SHE WAS about to pop one of her sticky toffees into my mouth. And I couldn't stand that, so I leaped out of bed, and it may have looked as though I was going to eat her or something. Then she started screaming.

"WOLF! WOLF!
You've eaten my grandma!"

Do I *look* the sort of wolf
who goes around eating grandmas?

IT GOT WORSE. The door swung open. There was a woodman there the size of a tree.

With an axe!

I shouted for help. But Grandma was still out cold in the wardrobe. She would tell you the truth. She really would.

The woodman took a swing at me, and I was *this* close to being a fur wrap!

I jumped out of that window, with the sound of the axe

CRASHING

down behind me.

I RAN ALL the way to town.
And I have to tell you — a wolf in a dress
is an embarrassed wolf! People were
laughing, and that's not nice.

Anyway, thanks for listening.
And, if you ever want any odd jobs
doing around the house, just get in touch.
Here's my card. I don't charge much, I'm a neat
worker, completely trustworthy, and,
I won't make a meal of it!

No, *please*. Look at me.
Would I lie to you?

WALKER BOOKS is the world's leading independent publisher of children's books. Working with the best authors and illustrators we create books for all ages, from babies to teenagers – books your child will grow up with and always remember. So…

FOR THE BEST CHILDREN'S BOOKS, LOOK FOR THE BEAR